⭐ FIRST FAIRY TALES ⭐

Rumpelstiltskin

For Natalie - *MM*
For Rufus - *PN*

Series reading consultant: Prue Goodwin,
Reading and Language Information Centre,
University of Reading

Orchard Books
96 Leonard Street, London EC2A 4XD
Orchard Books Australia
32/45-51 Huntley Street, Alexandria, NSW 2015
This text was first published in Great Britain in the form
of a gift collection called *First Fairy Tales*,
illustrated by Selina Young, in 1994
This edition first published in Great Britain in hardback in 2002
First paperback publication 2003
Text © Margaret Mayo 2002
Illustrations © Philip Norman 2002
The rights of Margaret Mayo to be identified as the author and
Philip Norman to be identified as the illustrator have been
asserted by them in accordance with the
Copyright, Designs and Patents Act, 1988.
A CIP catalogue record for this book is available from the British Library
ISBN 1 84121 140 0 (hardback)
ISBN 1 84121 152 4 (paperback)
1 3 5 7 9 10 8 6 4 2
1 3 5 7 9 10 8 6 4 2
Printed in Hong Kong, China

FIRST FAIRY TALES

Rumpelstiltskin

Margaret Mayo ⭐ Philip Norman

ORCHARD BOOKS

Once upon a time, there was a foolish farmer who had a beautiful clever daughter.

One day, the farmer went to the palace and started to show off. He said to the king, "I have a beautiful daughter!"

But the king took no notice. So the farmer said, "And she's clever! She can...SPIN STRAW INTO GOLD!"

Now, the king loved gold.
"Oh-ho!" he said. "I'd like to see
your daughter!"

So, the farmer hurried home and told his daughter that the king wanted to see her.

But, when the girl got to the palace, the king took her to a room where there was a pile of straw and a spinning-wheel.

"Spin this straw into gold!" he said.

And off he went.

The girl didn't know what to do, and she began to cry...

but then, a strange little man jumped in through the window.

"Beautiful girl," he said, "why are you crying?"

"I must spin this straw into gold," she answered. "And I don't know how to do it."

"What will you give me," said the little man, "if I do it for you?"

"My necklace," she said. And she gave it to him.

The little man sat down. The spinning-wheel whirled round and round, and the straw was spun into gold.

Then, with a skip and a jump, he was gone.

When the king saw the gold, he was pleased. But he wanted more. So, he took the girl to a room where there was a bigger pile of straw.

"Spin this straw into gold!" he said.

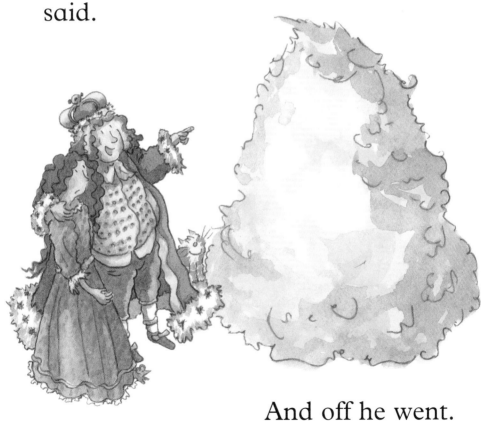

And off he went.

Again, the girl began to cry…
and then, the strange little man
jumped in through the window.

"More straw!" he said. "What
will you give me if I spin it for
you?"

"My ring," she said. And she
gave it to him.

Again, the spinning-wheel whirled round and round, and the straw was spun into gold. Then, with a skip and a jump, he was gone.

When the king saw the gold, he was very pleased. But he wanted even *more*. So, he took the girl to a room where there was an even bigger pile of straw. It reached right to the ceiling!

"Spin this straw into gold!" he said.

And off he went.

Again, the girl began to cry...
and then, the strange little man
jumped in through the window.

"Even more straw!" he said.
"What will you give me if I spin it
for you?"

"I have nothing left," said the
girl, sadly.

"Then promise," he said, "that when you are queen, you will give me your first little baby."

"Oh!" she said. "All right...I promise."

Once again, the spinning-wheel whirled round and round, and the straw was spun into gold. Then, with a skip and a jump, the little man was gone.

When the king saw the gold, he was very, very pleased. He thought, "This girl is clever and beautiful!"

So, he asked her to marry him, and the farmer's daughter became the queen.

A year passed by, and the queen had a baby. She had forgotten her promise to the little man.

But the little man had not forgotten. One day, he jumped in through the window.

"Now you must give me your baby," he said.

"Oh, no!" she said. "I'll give you jewels...a castle...anything. But not my baby."

"The baby is what I want," he said.

The queen began to cry, and
the little man was sorry for her.

He said, "If you can guess my
name, you can keep your baby. I
will give you three days and three
guesses each day."

As soon as the little man had
gone, the queen sent servants all
over the land to collect lots of
different names.

When the little man came back
the next day, she said, "Is your
name Caspar? Is it Jehoshaphat? Is
it Balthazar?"

But to each one, he said, "No!
That's not my name!"

On the second day, the queen said, "Is your name Skinny-legs? Is it Rumble-tummy? Is it Beaky-nose?"

But, to each one, the little man said, "No! That's not my name!"

On the morning of the third day, the queen was worried. She only had three guesses left. Then, one of the servants told her that he had seen a strange little man skipping round a fire in the forest. He was singing this song:

"Around and around,
I dance and I sing,
And nobody knows
I'm Rumpelstiltskin!"

The queen clapped her hands.
"That's his name!" she cried.
"Rumpelstiltskin!"

When the little man came for the last time, the queen said:

"I wonder...is your name... John?"

"No!" he laughed. "That's not my name!"

"I wonder..." she said, "could it be...Tom?"

"No! No!" he laughed. "That's not my name!"

"Well..." said the queen, "is it...
Rumpelstiltskin?"

"Who told you?" he shouted.
"Who? Who?"

He was so angry, he stamped a
hole in the floor, and whooshed
through it! And he was never seen
again.

Then, the queen picked up her baby, and she gave her lovely baby a great big happy hug!

FIRST FAIRY TALES
by Margaret Mayo
Illustrated by Philip Norman

Enjoy a little more magic with these First Fairy Tales:

❑ Cinderella   1 84121 138 9   £8.99

❑ Hansel and Gretel   1 84121 136 2   £8.99

❑ Jack and the Beanstalk   1 84121 134 6   £8.99

❑ Sleeping Beauty   1 84121 132 X   £8.99

❑ Rumpelstiltskin   1 84121 140 0   £8.99

❑ Snow White   1 84121 142 7   £8.99

Colour Crackers
by Rose Impey
Illustrated by Shoo Rayner

Have you read any Colour Crackers?

❑ A Birthday for Bluebell   1 84121 860 X   £7.99

❑ Hot Dog Harris   1 84121 864 2   £7.99

❑ Tiny Tim   1 84121 862 6   £7.99

❑ Too Many Babies   1 84121 866 9   £7.99

and many other titles.

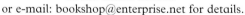

First Fairy Tales and Colour Crackers are available from all good bookshops, or can be ordered direct from the publisher:
Orchard Books, PO BOX 29, Douglas IM99 1BQ
Credit card orders please telephone 01624 836000
or fax 01624 837033
or e-mail: bookshop@enterprise.net for details.

To order please quote title, author and ISBN
and your full name and address.
Cheques and postal orders should be
made payable to 'Bookpost plc'.
Postage and packing is FREE within the UK
(overseas customers should add £1.00 per book).

Prices and availability are subject to change.